KIDS' SPORTS STORIES

T-BALL TURNAROUND

by Elliott Smith

illustrated by Amanda Erb

PICTURE WINDOW BOOKS
a capstone imprint

Published by Picture Window Books, an imprint of Capstone
1710 Roe Crest Drive, North Mankato, Minnesota 56003
capstonepub.com

Library of Congress Cataloging-in-Publication Data is available
on the Library of Congress website.
ISBN: 9781666338966 (hardcover)
ISBN: 9781666338973 (paperback)
ISBN: 9781666338980 (ebook PDF)

Summary: Alex wants to try T-ball. But he's nervous about meeting new
kids and learning the game. At first, he's so worried he doesn't even go
on the field. With the help of a new friend, Alex starts to build his baseball
skills and gain confidence. But he still worries about what the other
players think of him. Will Alex be able to control his nerves with the game
on the line?

Editorial Credits
Editor: Carrie Sheely; Designer: Bobbie Nuytten; Media Researcher:
Morgan Walters; Production Specialist: Polly Fisher

Printed and bound in the USA. PO4882

TABLE OF CONTENTS

Glossary

 **dugout**—the place where T-ball teams sit when not playing

 **grounder**—a ball hit on the ground

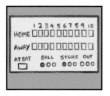 **inning**—a part of a T-ball game with a turn at bat for each team

 **pop fly**—a short hit into the air

 **tee**—a pole used in T-ball; the ball sits on top of the tee

Chapter 1
NERVES

Alex sat on his bed. He had a baseball in one hand and his worry stone in the other. His mom had given him the stone. It was smooth and colorful. She told him it could help when he was worried. Alex used it a lot. Now, he was nervous about starting T-ball.

"You almost ready?" Alex's dad asked.

"I don't know," Alex said. "What if my team doesn't like me?"

"Just be yourself, and they'll like you," Dad said. "Focus on having fun!"

Alex arrived at practice. Kids threw balls back and forth. Alex started to worry.

"What's wrong?" said a smiling girl. "I'm Lillian. Do you want to throw with me?"

Alex felt like his feet couldn't move. "Uh, not right now," he said.

"Hello, everyone!" a man said. "My name is Coach Dillon. Our team is the Crushers. We're going to learn how to play T-ball. Let's get on the field!"

The other players ran out onto the field. But Alex was too nervous. He stayed on the bench. He didn't want to make any mistakes. Coach walked up to Alex. "It's okay, Alex," Coach said. "Come out when you're ready."

When Alex looked up, he saw some kids on the field whispering. Alex knew they were talking about him! He felt even worse.

Coach set up a **tee**. The kids took turns hitting the ball. Alex thought it looked fun. Lillian got a hit and waved to Alex. One kid named Miller hit the ball far.

When practice ended, Alex walked
slowly to his dad's car. "See you next
time!" Lillian shouted.

Chapter 2
FINDING COURAGE

At home, Alex told his parents why he didn't go out on the field. "I understand," Mom said. "Remember, everyone has to learn when they start. All you can do is your best, and that's always enough."

The next practice day came. Alex remembered what his mom had said. He put his worry stone in the back pocket of his baseball pants. That would help too.

When he got to the field, Lillian ran over. "Let's play together," she said.

"That would be great," Alex said.

Lillian showed Alex how to use two hands to catch **pop flies**. Other players said hi. Alex started to relax.

Coach Dillon gathered the team to practice hitting. Soon, it was Alex's turn.

Alex walked to the tee. He took a deep breath and swung. WHOOSH! He missed the ball! Alex felt a moment of panic. But no one was laughing.

"Nice try!" Coach said.

The rest of practice went well. Alex was practicing baserunning when he felt his worry stone fall out. Miller picked it up.

"What's this?" he asked as several players looked on.

Alex gulped. "It's, uh, my worry stone," he said. "It helps me when I get nervous."

Miller nodded and handed it back. Alex was embarrassed. The best player on the team knew he was scared!

At the end of practice, Coach told the team the first game was Saturday.

Chapter 3

THE BIG CATCH

On the day of the game, Alex was getting ready when his mom came into his room. "Are you excited about the game?" she asked.

"I am, but also a little nervous," he said.

"It's normal to feel that way before trying something new," she said. "You'll do great."

Alex arrived at the field to see a big
crowd. Lillian came over and gave him a
high five. In the **dugout**, Alex took the
worry stone out of his pocket. Miller sat
next to him.

"Hey, can I see your stone?" Miller asked.
"I'm pretty nervous. I don't want to strike
out."

Alex was shocked. How could Miller be worried? "I'm nervous too," Alex said. "But I'm going to try hard."

Alex set the stone on the dugout railing. Before long, every member of the team had touched it. Alex felt a lot better knowing he wasn't the only one who was nervous.

The game started. His first time batting, Alex hit a **grounder** to third base. He was thrown out at first but wasn't upset. The game went back and forth. The Crushers were winning 6-5 in the last **inning**.

"Okay, Crushers, one more out!" Lillian shouted.

Alex secretly hoped no one would hit the ball to him at second base.

But the Eagles' batter swung and hit a
high **pop fly** right to him! Before Alex could
even think, he put up his glove and other
hand like Lillian had showed him. The ball
plopped into his glove. The Crushers won!

"Great job!" Lillian shouted. Alex smiled as the team jumped all around him.

FEED THE ALLIGATOR

Try this drill to practice fielding grounders. It will help you learn to use both hands to keep the ball in your glove.

What You Need:
- ball
- glove
- a friend

What You Do:
- Stand on flat ground about 10 feet (3 meters) away from your friend.
- Take turns rolling the ball to each other. When receiving the ball, put your glove on the ground and your other hand above it. The glove is the "mouth" of the alligator.
- As the ball goes into the glove, use your other hand to "feed" the alligator. Close it on the ball as it enters your glove.

REPLAY IT

Think about when Miller shared with Alex that he was nervous before the game. How do you think this made Alex feel? Write about a time when you were nervous. What helped you feel better? Alex rubs a stone to help himself relax. Some people take deep breaths or write down how they are feeling. Find out what works for you!

ABOUT THE AUTHOR

Elliott Smith is a former sports reporter who covered athletes in all sports from high school to the pros. He is one of the authors of the Natural Thrills series about extreme outdoor sports. In his spare time, he likes playing sports with his two children, going to the movies, and adding to his collection of Pittsburgh Steelers memorabilia.

ABOUT THE ILLUSTRATOR

Amanda Erb is an illustrator from Maryland currently living in the Boston, Massachusetts, area. She earned a BFA in illustration from Ringling College of Art and Design. In her free time, she enjoys playing soccer, learning Spanish, and discovering new stories to read.